# SAVE THE PRINCESS

Mike Dionne

Copyright © 2013, 2014, 2022, 2023 by Mike Dionne

All rights reserved. No part of this book may be reproduced or used in any manner without written permission of the copyright owner, except for the use of quotations in a book review.

Book cover and drawings by Sean Farquhar

First paperback edition October 2022

ISBN 979-8361332748 (paperback)

# INTRODUCTION: THE KINGDOM OF ANTONIA

The road into the mountains was not as treacherous as many of the soldiers had believed. Superstition had kept them from venturing into the mountains, but they reached the foothills without incident. Even the goblins did not stop them. But once they reached the end of the trees, it became dangerous. Some soldiers slipped and fell into ravines so deep that they seemed to have no bottom. Boulders crashed down on others, perhaps moved by goblins, perhaps not. But soon King Anthony spotted the Goblin King's fortress at the top of the highest peak, at the crest of the mountain ring.

They climbed again with greater fervor, certain that the princess was held inside the fortress. When they reached the top, they came to the entrance, only to find it surrounded by a great moat. The bridge across was so wide they began to wonder what it was meant for. Within seconds, they had their answer.

A great green dragon flew over the bridge and landed hard on the ground in front of it. The ground shook hard enough for some of the soldiers to fall over. Scrambling, they drew back, taking cover behind rocks as the dragon unleashed a jet of flame.

The archers drew the dragon's attention with volleys of arrows, and the king's men begged him to go on and find his daughter. As the sun went down, he waited for the dragon to turn away and ran by it as it protected its head from more arrows. He pushed open the great doors of the fortress, which immediately slammed shut behind him.

King Anthony looked around in the dim light and saw nothing.

The last remaining sunlight came in through small windows on a staircase up ahead. He stopped when he heard the sound of high-pitched laughter, but continued on.

Outside, he could see down into the mountain valley. It was a barren wasteland; nothing but a rocky field. Firelight showed that it was filled to the brim with goblins holding torches and looking up patiently, waiting for something.

His daughter screamed, and he ran up the stairs, sword in hand. At the top of the stairs he was greeted by a dozen goblins, leaping at him. He cut some down with his sword but most climbed on him. Kicking, he tried to break free, but they were all over him. Lunging, he crushed three goblins between his back and the stone wall. Falling and rolling he put enough distance between himself and the remaining goblins to kick them or strike them with his sword.

As he pressed on goblins came at him one or two at a time, and he never let them get close. He grew weary of the little defense they'd put up. With his daughter still alive, he was certain they could not have counted only on the dragon to protect them.

He entered the throne room and saw only one thing: his daughter, strapped to a table under a circular, open roof. When he reached her side he put a hand to her face.

Dazed, her eyes fluttered as she woke. She was covered in dirt and bruises. "Father? Father, is that really you?"

"Yes. Yes, we're going home." He smiled.

Her eyes grew wide with fear, and she began to struggle against the ropes that held her in place. "Father, you have to watch out for him. He is very powerful."

"Who?" Just then he was struck hard in the back by a candlestick. He turned to see a goblin larger than any he'd seen, though standing only four feet high. On his head was a great gold crown. His sharp teeth gleamed in a murderous smile. This was the Goblin King.

He readied his sword for another attack, but the Goblin King had no weapon. Rushing forward to attack, the creature merely moved his hands, but King Anthony was caught off guard when another candlestick struck him from behind. Objects began to fly at him from all sides now. He could do little more than cover his head with his arms.

Sophia gasped. "Father, watch out!" He spun around but to no avail; a spear struck him in the shoulder and he fell to his knees. Another flew at him, striking him in the belly. Wailing, he fell over.

Ignoring him now, the Goblin King climbed to a podium at one end of the table where Sophia was held. Outside the goblins began to chant; the full moon had risen. He pulled on a rope and gears began to move in the wall; a great red crystal was raised into place directly above Sophia. Flipping the pages of a huge book he began to read, screaming in his own language. Suddenly light from the moon was focused into a beam that went right through Sophia's heart. She screamed.

King Anthony, unable to stand, did all he could to turn toward Sophia. He did not think he would be able to crawl to her in time. Summoning the last of his strength against the worst pain he'd ever felt, he took his sword in his hand and threw it like a spear at the Goblin King. Struck through the heart, the Goblin King exploded into a cloud of dust. The beam from the crystal disappeared.

King Anthony now crawled close enough to Sophia to untie one of her hands. When she'd freed herself, she rushed to his side. Crying, she took his head in her hands. The room began to shake; dust began to fall from the ceiling. Wood cracked as both the table and podium collapsed.

"Sophia, you need to go now."

She shook her head, her eyes closed. "I won't leave you!"

"You must. There is no saving me now. I came here to get you back and I have done that. Think of your mother. She will need you now. Go. Go and find the soldiers."

She embraced him one last time and fled as the entire room collapsed behind her. Running down the stairs, dust filled the air as soldiers rushed in. They led her outside and asked about the king. She explained.

One of the soldiers stepped forward. "He just turned to dust? That could explain the dragon." Many soldiers nodded.

Sophia looked at them, confused.

"One moment we were fighting the dragon, the next, it was just...gone. We didn't defeat it. The beast just disappeared. Perhaps it was part of some spell."

Exhausted, they camped for the night, planning to make their way home the following morning. When she woke, Sophia looked out upon the Valley of the Goblins to see that the goblins were gone, and the wasteland had been transformed into a valley lush with trees. In the center a Great Lake, which we know as Lake Anthony, fed into a river, and along its banks grew groves of fruit trees. It was paradise.

The queen grieved for her husband, but Sophia convinced her that his death had not been in vain. Not only were the goblins gone, but their people could live in paradise if they so wished. The queen could not bring herself to leave, but soon after Sophia led a large group of people from Fortuna, many of them young, into the mountains to build a new life in the valley.

Abandoning the Goblin Fortress they built a new castle on Lake Anthony, and she declared the new Kingdom of Antonia in honor of her father. Beloved as a queen, she ruled over a land of peace and prosperity. With only a single road through the mountains, Antonia has been safe from invasion ever since. And that, children, is how our land was founded."

The teacher, whose hair was gray at a very early age, closed the storybook and sighed as a small boy with dark hair rolled his eyes. "What is it now, Unter?"

Unter, ten years old but very small for his age, cleared his throat before speaking. "That story makes no sense."

"How many times have you heard this story, Unter?"

"From you, ma'am, I count seventy-two times."

She raised her eyebrows. "And it suddenly makes no sense at all?"

"Well, honestly, I never thought about some of the details before. King Anthony, for example. If he was hurt so badly, how did he have the strength to throw his sword?"

She pursed her lips. "Well, Unter, many men are capable of great strength when those they love are in danger. Your own father lifted a cart all by himself when it turned over and fell on his brother."

Unter nodded. "Well then, what about the crystal and the magic book?"

"What about them?"

"Did they just disappear when the spell was broken, like the dragon?"

"I don't know Unter. Maybe. Most of the fortress collapsed and was abandoned."

"So they could still be inside?"

"I suppose it's possible, Unter. But the goblins and their magic are gone. It's been nearly a thousand years since the day the spell was broken, but what matters is that the collapsed fortress is very dangerous. It's close to the borderlands and no one ventures there, not even the soldiers." She looked at all of the children. "Remember how dangerous it is, children. The fortress has loose stones even to this day, and playing around in there could get you crushed."

The widow Cassandra dismissed the children for the day. Unter left alone, as he always did.

# THE RIDER IN BLACK

The sound of hoof beats in the darkness carried far down the road out of the mountains and into the forest. Only a few would take that road at night, and only the bravest of those would take it on a moonless night. Fewer still would ride at such a casual pace. The rider feared nothing in the forest. A timber wolf howled; the rider and his horse pressed on. The great black horse showed no strain. He'd made this ride many times before and returned home with no more effort than a walk around his stable. Despite the casual pace, however, the rider was in more of a hurry than ever before. This was the most important meeting. He had to be on time, and the meeting had to go exactly as planned.

The tavern was the only light for miles, and only one of the windows was lit. Though he wasn't late, the soldiers arrived first, and he didn't like it. He scoffed as he dismounted and led his horse to the stable. The stable boy, whose wide eyes and curly hair gave him a comical look, reached for the reigns and held a palm up. The rider produced two silver coins and dropped one into the boy's palm; when the boy reached for the other, he closed his fist on it. Once the stable boy had cowered sufficiently, the rider smiled and flipped the other coin in the air, walking away as the boy leapt for it eagerly.

He entered the candlelit tavern and walked past the owner without acknowledgement. The General was already seated, two of his lieutenants standing nearby, trying to look intimidating. He left his hood up and smiled as he sat.

"You're eager, Foster. That's good. You have good reason to be."

Foster frowned. "I am getting a little tired of hearing that I'll have the information soon, Golamel. So, if this is another one of your vague developments, you'd better not expect me to get excited about it this time."

"After tonight we won't have to meet again. I have everything you need. Everything."

Foster only glared at him. "Well then, let's have it."

From under his cloak, Golamel produced a bundle of papers. "Everything. A map of the kingdom with outposts. Troop numbers, shift changes at the castle. Your men will need to know where to be when you attack."

"I don't see why I need to sacrifice perfectly good troops with this attack. We can't take the kingdom by force, not even with our superior numbers."

"And you don't have to. The attack will be a diversion. The castle guard will rush out to fight the army while your men subdue the few that remain to raid the treasury. With all of that gold you can hire enough mercenaries to swell your numbers further still, and return with a much larger force that will be large enough to take the kingdom in broad daylight."

"And you? What do you get out of this? Did the king make fun of that big nose of yours?"

Golamel scowled. "That entire kingdom deserves to suffer. They have resources and land you want, and when you take them, the people there will be crushed under your feet. And I will smile."

# THE MILLER'S SON

Unter's family lived in the house next to the mill. His father, Cassius, ran the mill and his mother, Helen, ran the household. Every day Unter walked alone to the widow Cassandra's home for school, then back to the bend in the river where his family lived.

His oldest brother, Cassius the Younger, already worked at the mill. The twins, Apollo and Artemis, had finished their schooling. Much of his mother's attention went to caring for the baby, his younger sister, Penelope.

Unter returned every day without fanfare. Helen often entertained guests already trying to arrange marriages to the twins, prized for their beauty through the entire kingdom. Often, she would say that Penelope, too, would likely get the same good looks, to which all would respond that they came from Helen, who would act quite flattered.

On that day there was no company at home, but things went as usual. His mother was feeding the baby as a pot of stew boiled over the fire, and the twins were having one of their common boasting matches.

"Well," began Artemis, "all I know is that Harold couldn't keep his eyes off me, and James spent the entire day trying to get my attention, even though his parents have had their minds made up that he's going to marry Gwendolyn since they were born on the same day."

"Well," answered Apollo, "you're a girl, and boys are supposed to try and woo you. I have girls coming after me all the time and they're not even supposed to do that. I didn't have to do any of my schoolwork for the past three years between Deborah, Joan and

Maggie. But today was really something. Nadia ran all the way to the stables and asked if she could help me finish my chores. Do you believe that? A girl helping with the manual labor!"

Helen interrupted. "You'd better not have any ideas about that Nadia. Her father is a farm hand. If anything happened between you two then you'd be out on your own with no dowry and that means your father would be stuck with the debt for your first expenses, or worse, you'd be living here. You're better off--when the time comes and not until--marrying Carmen. After all her father is the cobbler and is, as commoners go, well-to-do. He's not the richest in town but he is the richest man with a daughter that doesn't look like her family tree is made of trolls." Artemis giggled.

"Mother, she's insufferable! Not to mention she's completely taken with the cooper's boy and so all she ever talks about are shoes and barrels."

Artemis smiled slyly. "Well, the cooper's boy is Max and I can tell you that he is quite taken with someone else."

Helen put the baby down for a nap. "I don't know about that Max either, young lady. His family may have money but they have quite the reputation. I understand his father and his father's father both walked to the altar at knifepoint, and had babies not exactly nine months later. I will not have our family's good name soiled with that lot." She began stirring the pot, and looked puzzled. "Where is your father? He should have been home some time ago. Apollo, will run to the mill and--"

Cassius the Younger burst in the door, his huge shoulders heaving. He was covered in mud.

Helen dropped the spoon. "What is it? Where is your father?"

Cassius gasped for breath. "They've called us out to fight. Cavalry is approaching on the road. Father sent me for the armor. When I get back, we'll help building a defensive blockade."

Apollo stood up. "Am I going with you?"

"You most certainly are not!" Helen's eyes were wide, now angry rather than frightened. "If there's a war, you'll be called. If you're called, you'll go, then and not a moment sooner, do you hear me?"

Apollo lowered his eyes, suddenly looking much younger. "Yes, ma'am."

Cassius loaded the armor into a wooden hand cart, and left.

# THE GAMBIT

It had taken six days, but Golamel and the small regiment reached the edge of the valley, and waited for the signal. Nearly everything had already gone according to the plan. They'd made camp in plenty of time, nearly a full day before the assault was to take place. It had taken a lot of convincing, but Foster had finally agreed to the assault if he could load up on archers. This, Foster believed, would minimize his losses. The assault was going to be a failure, but it would buy his men enough time to rob the Antonian treasury in the castle, which would be left with minimal protection.

What Golamel needed now was for the signal, a flaming arrow, to be fired at the correct time, and for his messenger to arrive exactly at the time agreed upon. Timing was crucial for the entire plan. If anything happened too late now, or possibly worse, too early, his plans would be ruined and his goals so much more difficult to attain. Nevertheless, he was confident.

As the sun went down, they moved past the tree line and within sight of the castle. The captain wanted to move in when they saw the first group of castle guards heading out, but Golamel insisted they wait. Four more regiments headed out before full dark. The few remaining sentries abandoned their posts on the castle walls. Then he told them to watch the skies.

"Right on time." The arrow was an orange dot against the black sky, distinct from the stars in both color and motion. Golamel nodded to the captain. The troops crouched and headed toward the rear castle wall.

Golamel waited patiently until the last of the soldiers had climbed the wall, and let a few seconds pass. Then he threw their ropes over the top of the wall and moved around the corner of the outer wall. He came to a small door with a large metal lock, and extended his right hand in a fist, first turning his wrist palm up, then opening his hand so that his fingers pointed at the lock. It fell open; he walked inside and the door locked behind him.

He hurried through the narrow corridors. He was quite certain that his messenger was on time, but just for the time being, it didn't matter. He came to a winding stone staircase and ran up, knowing it led into the south tower, far from the treasury near the dungeon where the soldiers were packing up the gold.

He came to another heavy wooden door, with a barred window but unlocked. He looked through the window and saw the castle guards he expected, both looking quite bored and a little sleepy.           Looking at them through the bars of the small window, he held up his hands with his palms toward them, then closed them into tight fists. The guards disappeared, replaced by two tiny white mice that ran down the corridor.

He casually swung open the door. The princess turned over in her bed, sleepy. Her eyes grew wide and she opened her mouth to scream, when he raised his hands up and swung them back down quickly. She closed her eyes and fell sideways, asleep. He unrolled a large brown sack.

Smiling as he went, he slunk down the corridor with the full sack over his shoulder. As he left the castle he looked around; there was no sign of the soldiers. In the distance he saw torches approaching and moved as quickly as he could for the tree line.

# MIKE DIONNE

# SEARCH

Helen shook Unter awake. "Get ready. We all need to help search for the princess."

"What happened?"

"Your father and brother came home last night just fine. The invading army was routed. It was all a ruse to try and rob the castle. The guards caught all the thieves, but the princess was missing. Everyone's searching the entire kingdom. No more school for you, at least until we find her."

Unter dressed in a hurry. He knew that with the princess in danger, it wasn't right to feel excited, but he'd never heard of anything half as interesting happening while he was alive. Helen gathered up the baby and Cassius led the other children out the door and up the road.

They walked up the hill and toward the castle. It was a long walk, one that Unter would have been happy to take alone at his own pace, but his father was almost running. Helen, carrying the baby, had the hardest time keeping up. Everyone was very tired and no one spoke. Eventually, Cassius began to slow down, hearing Helen grunting repeatedly as she switched the baby from one arm to the other. He crossed his arms to show his reluctance.

When they reached the castle, the sun was still hidden behind it. A large crowd had gathered, but much of the kingdom was still on the way.            The king and queen stood on the wall above the main gate, both looking very grave. The blank look on the queen's face reminded Unter of the time a man had died working at the mill. The man's wife had come to see if he would survive his injuries, but it had been too late; after she knew he was dead, she had the same blank look of despair on her face.

As the sun began to show above the castle walls the king waddled to the parapets and cleared his throat. The crowd went silent in anticipation. "As you may all know by now," he said, voice booming, "our kingdom has endured a great tragedy. Last night we were invaded, and our army turned back those invaders, just as they always have. At the same time, an attempt was made to rob our treasury. Castle guards returned in time to stop the robbery, but it seems that both the invasion and the robbery were part of a devious ruse."

"Princess Sophia is missing. We suspect that the forces of the Lowland Kingdoms are to blame. But whoever took the princess did not leave the kingdom. After they left the castle, they did not escape on the road through the mountains, which was heavily guarded following the invasion attempt. We believe Sophia is alive, and being held captive somewhere inside the kingdom. I have a great task to ask of you, my subjects. Return my daughter to me. My guards alone are not enough to search the entire kingdom, small as it may be. We need your help to find her. Please, return to your homes, those places you know best. Anywhere you think they might have her hidden, look there. If you find anything at all please find the nearest guard. Whoever took Sophia bested her bodyguards. They are dangerous, and I cannot and will not ask you to put yourselves in harm's way. But please… find her."

The king let out a long sigh and turned away from the crowd. Unter let out a sigh of his own. "So, we had to walk all this way to be told to go home?"

Several people looked at him. Helen shot him an angry look. "Unter! Hush!" The people around shrugged in agreement.

The family, already tired and upset, began the long walk back. Castle guards were everywhere. Most seemed to be searching the castle grounds and moving outward, while others were aimless. One very tall guard bent over and picked up a rock the size of a rabbit. Then he looked underneath it. Unter rolled his eyes.

A few of the families headed home ran with enthusiasm, as if they knew where she was and would win a prize when they'd found her. But most of the families looked as dejected as Unter's. They'd been woken before dawn and asked to walk to the castle, when they could have been told to search at home immediately. It had been a waste of time tempered only by the sorrow of the king and queen.

They stopped at the mill before returning home. Cassius doubted the kidnappers had hidden there, but they searched it all anyway. Again, after they returned home, they searched the house they'd just left, knowing no one had been there. Apollo even climbed under the house, but found nothing. They left the neighboring families to search their own property, and looked around. There was nothing but houses, the mill, and a few lonely trees. The land was flat all the way to the mountain rim, where the pines started to grow thick again.

Helen was angry and tired, the baby was fussy, and Cassius was visibly frustrated. He told Helen to take Unter and the girls and go home. He would take the older boys, gather the neighbors and search the nearby forest until dark.

Helen put the baby down for a nap. They all sat around the fire not saying much until it was time to start dinner. It wasn't quite dark and dinner was not quite ready when Cassius and the boys burst in the door. Cassius slammed the door shut behind them. Their faces were covered in soot and they were gasping for air.

Helen dropped the spoon in her hand. "What happened?"

Cassius caught enough breath to sputter, "Dragon."

She looked at him skeptically. "There hasn't been a dragon near here since the settlement. The ones that remained fled north, past troll lands."

Apollo spoke up. "It was a dragon alright. We were lucky, we didn't get close. The trees caught fire, and we ran all the way home."

Helen sat and sighed. She shook her head and placed a hand over her heart. "You three wash up for supper."

All through supper, Unter's mind raced. He kept coming back to the story of the kingdom's settlement: a missing princess named Sophia, a dragon, lots of unusual occurrences. All at once he knew what he had to do.

While the rest of the family sat around the table, he started gathering supplies. It would be cold in the mountains, so he made sure he had his warmest fur, and a hat. He packed the blankets he'd used on the long trip for supplies he'd taken with his father the year before, as well as bread, cheese and a waterskin. At last, he strapped on the knife his grandfather had given him, despite his mother's protests.

He walked to the door and turned to the table where his family still sat, rehashing the search and the dragon attack. "I'm going to save the princess," he said, reaching for the door handle. No one turned to look at him. "Make sure you stay close to the house if you're going to play outside," Helen said. Unter looked at them for a few seconds, then walked out the door.

# DIVERSIONS

Sophia looked out the window, staring at the pillars of smoke rising from the trees.

"Enjoying the show?" Golamel stood in the doorway. Sophia shivered. "The dragon's just the beginning. I've got a troll headed out, and more to follow."

She looked up at him. "Why? Why are you doing this?"

He narrowed his eyes and smiled at her. "Princess, you see right now a monster of a man, a criminal, a kidnapper, and now ultimately, a murderer. But this kingdom decided I was vile before I was anything at all. My mother took one look at my big nose and nearly threw me to the floor, as if her womb had borne rotted fruit. She named me Golamel. My brother's name was Fortimus. What kind of mother does that to a child? One can only live so long bearing the name of evil unearned. Before long, the idea of embracing that mantle becomes very attractive."

Sophia glared back at him. "So, you became evil because people assumed you would? Hardly earns you any sympathy."

Golamel's nostrils flared. "Who are you to lecture anyone? You're a pampered child who has lived a life of privilege. Have you ever had to make a decision for yourself? Has anyone dared insult you in your life?"

Sophia gulped hard. She didn't reply. In the distance she saw a dust cloud as some of the king's cavalry headed out of the castle gates. The ground shook, and the troll, club in hand, emerged from the trees. As it bellowed, the cavalry group turned and sped toward it.

She turned away from the window. "If you're so powerful, why not just destroy the kingdom? Isn't that what you want? Why not one fell swoop?"

Golamel now strode past Sophia to look out the window himself. "Destruction of this kingdom will happen soon enough, but you see, that's not my goal. It will only be a consequence. My goal is to show this kingdom pain. Just as slowly as possible, I want to give this kingdom as much pain as it has given me."

# THE QUEST BEGINS

Unter had struggled with the decision of whether or not to use the road on his quest, but ultimately, he stuck to it. It wasn't always the most direct route but whenever he strayed from it, he was surprised at how much his pace slowed. He'd only stopped once to nibble at some food. Water would be easy to come by for most of the journey. Rivers and streams were plentiful on the way; food would be another matter. Depending on strangers to provide it seemed not only bothersome, but a big gamble as well.

As night closed in, he paid little attention to the sounds in the distance, and started looking for a place to make shelter. He hadn't cared much for his father, nor his father for him, but Cassius had passed on some practical knowledge on the trips they'd taken in the wilderness. Unter hadn't wanted to go, but now he was glad. Cassius had shown him many things, but right now what he remembered best was caves.

It had been in the middle of winter; they had been walking for hours with no apparent direction, and all Unter wanted to do was stop somewhere so he could sleep by the fire. Cassius did something he did not expect. "Where should we make shelter, son?"

Unter froze; rarely did Cassius pay Unter any mind at all. To call him son, and to ask him a real question, was shocking. He looked around and saw a cave mouth in a nearby rock formation. "There," he said, pointing.

Cassius patted him on the head. "Good eye. Can we make a fire in there?"

Unter stopped to think. "We can bring wood in from outside. It should be dry on the inside, and big enough so we won't choke on the smoke."

"Yes, that's right. What else is in the cave?"

"What?"

"What else is in the cave? How big is the cave? How deep does it go?"

"I… I don't know."

"Good answer. You never know how deep a cave is, or what's in there. If we were the army, and we had torches, we might be able to search it through. Some caves are small, and not too deep. If animals were inside a small cave well, the army could spook them out, or even have them for dinner. But we are not an army. We have no torches. These forest caves usually have occupants. I doubt if you'll find a lost mountain troll in there, but you don't need to. Remember, if you fall asleep by the fire in a cave, the smoke can wake up animals living deep inside. Even a wild dog could kill you while you sleep, and would try, if you've come into his cave. An unknown cave is no safe place to sleep. That's why we need to make our own shelter. It's not as good at keeping the wind out, it's not as warm, it's not as dry, but we know what's in it. Us. Most animals will stay away, especially if there's a fire."

He had then helped his father make a lean-to shelter against the rocks, to clean the snow from the ground so they could make a fire, and to shore it up to protect against the wind. It had been hard work, and the shelter was only just warm enough, but they had made it through, and were never bothered by animals. And, sure enough, the next day they saw animal tracks in and out of the cave mouth.

Unter went about making his own fire and his own shelter. It had taken twice as long to make a shelter half the size without his father to help him, and the fire did not seem to warm him at all, but when he woke in the morning, he found that he was still alive, and that his shelter had held. Nibbling at food once again he headed for the stream to refill his waterskin.

# AN INVISIBLE THREAT

Unter followed the road, walking by day as quickly as he could. He knew that at night, he had to make a fire quickly not only to keep warm, but to keep the animals away. His father had taught him that wolves and bears would generally leave him alone during the day, but at night they would be more aggressive, especially without fire to keep them at bay. He passed many houses but most of the farmers seemed not to be home; he could not say if they'd locked themselves in, fled, or gone out to find the princess, as he had. Many groups of the king's soldiers passed, sometimes on horseback, sometimes on foot, but he merely stepped off the road as they passed. None seemed to notice him at all.

On the third day the sun came out in the afternoon, and it became unseasonably warm. Though he thought it would be smarter to press on and get as far as possible, he could not help himself. He sat down under a pine tree and made himself a lunch. Those birds that had not yet gone south flew low over the river, and he imagined how much he would enjoy being one of them right then, playing like small children while flying through the air.

He finished his food and packed up, but rather than moving on right away he sat back against the tree again, looking in all directions. This place was lovely; he could see the white caps of the furthest mountains, and it had neither the sounds nor the smells of the mill. He had thought this might be his favorite place in the whole kingdom. Dreams of a home here flooded in; a small house, with just enough room for him, a wood pile stacked neatly outside, and smoke spilling out of a stone chimney.

Screams sobered him; he looked around to see a heavily armed cavalry group running from the forest at the edge of the hills. Only a few horses remained, and a single rider broke from the group, speeding back toward the castle. The rest of the soldiers regrouped on the far side of the road, their backs to Unter, and weapons ready. The ground shook, and puffs of black smoke came out of the trees. Quite suddenly the dragon emerged. Its thick skin was a dark red, its four legs as thick as tree trunks. The snout was both long and wide, with flashes of fire from the nostrils. Atop its head was what appeared to be a mane of many colors; Unter could not tell if it was skin or hair or both. As it moved closer, he caught glimpses of its bright red tongue, forked and serpentine, which moved in and out of its mouth very quickly, but had to be at least two feet long. When it moved its head to one side, he saw a single great eye open, yellow and strange but at the same time more human than animal.

The soldiers froze in place. For a moment the dragon also stopped just in front of the trees. Then it lowered its head and charged, the ground rumbling, and it spread its great wings and leapt into the air. The soldiers shivered. The dragon turned, heading away from them, but flipped in mid-air and turned back to flank them, moving as if it were in water rather than air. Flames came upon them like jets and the soldiers screamed and broke ranks; Unter stared at the dragon, who looked back at them and appeared to laugh.

The dragon seemed content to dive at the soldiers over and over, to wait for them to form ranks and break them from all angles, to spray them with flames and watch them run away frightened. Even these, the best of the king's soldiers, seemed no threat to it. The beast was toying with them.

Unter decided it was time to leave. He gathered his things and walked along the road. The dragon could have seen him, and he was sure he'd made eye contact at least once, but it paid no attention. When he'd made his way up the road and looked back, the soldiers had all formed up and headed back toward the castle, with the dragon pursuing casually.

That evening he experienced a similar situation with a group of farmers armed with pitchforks; they were taking on the troll, who had demolished many homes. It was immensely tall, at least twenty feet, its thick skin the gray of dull iron. The troll carried a club that was at least ten feet long. Some of the farmers threw their pitchforks but most poked at the air in front of them as if trying to shoo the troll away. Each swing was powerful but both slow and predictable; the troll grunted loudly before each swing, and each time the farmers seemed to be ready for it, running out of the way and stabbing the troll as it followed through, then running way again. Neither the farmers nor the troll appeared to notice Unter at all.

That night as he made a fire, Unter thought happily about the chances of his quest; he expected that his good luck would continue. Whatever force had taken the princess would not consider him at all. Evil would underestimate him, dismissing his small size. He began to wonder if accomplishing his task would be easier than he'd ever imagined. The king would be pleased, perhaps the royal family would even build that little house by the river he now wanted so badly.

It simply did not occur to him to think that a small boy would fail to save the princess. His age and size were not assets to him, but he did not see them as weaknesses either. If things continued as they had he would simply walk in unimpeded, and facing whatever evil force had taken the prisoner would be his first and only real challenge. His classmates that snickered at him for being different would then embrace him as if they'd loved him all along, falling all over each other to praise him. And he would leave them behind, living a peaceful life alone in his house by the river.

That night, though the wind howled outside, the warmth of the afternoon gone, he slept better than ever, as if he were already safe and warm inside his house.

# BUMP IN THE ROAD

He awoke in the morning refreshed and happy to be alive. Casually, as if he were alone at home, he woke up and walked outside, stretching his arms above him. He got ready to head for the nearest stream so that he could fill his waterskin. After he walked past the remaining embers of his fire, he saw it and froze.

The wolf was majestic. It was as tall as he was, or would be if it stopped sniffing the ground and stood up straight. The fur was thick and shiny, so dark that it seemed to be blacker than black, a purple-blue. His father's lessons returned to him again and though he still could not make himself move he realized that he was downwind and the wolf smelled something, but not him. For the moment he was safe; the wolf had not seen nor heard him.

Unter closed his eyes and willed himself to move. Slowly he crept backward without a sound, back toward the shelter, not knowing what he would do with his knife if the wolf attacked. Still the wolf did not look up, he was nearly there, when... CRACK.

A twig snapped beneath his feet. The wolf looked up suddenly. For a half second it remained a thing of beauty and grace, almost otherworldly in its perfection. Then it was down, fur bristled, body tense, white teeth bared in a snarl. Now the shelter seemed a mile away and he did not know what to do. He ran for the fire, hoping to grab the remnants of a log to use as a weapon, but he did not get there. The wolf leapt and Unter raised his hands, pushing the waterskin and his fur out in front of himself. The wolf chomped down on his fur and seemed to become enraged, shaking it from side to side.

Unter lost his balance and they fell together. The heavier wolf pushed down on him and he moved sideways, turning, and he felt himself fall onto the wolf's hot belly. He was free; the force had caused the wolf to let go of the fur, so he was on the ground, and turned to find the wolf, who also turned to look at him. Then it looked away and began to wail in pain.

His ears rang; the noises were so loud he clapped his hands to the sides of his head, forgetting the threat of the wolf for a moment. It rolled away from him, out of the fire, and continued rolling on the ground. Stumbling, it got to its feet and ran, never looking back.

Standing up, Unter gathered himself, breathing heavily and looking around. There were no other animals nearby and he did not expect there would be. He sat on the ground and hugged his knees, and that's when he began to cry. Crying, in Unter's experience, was something the other school children did to get the teacher's attention. Claudius called Delilah ugly, so she cried. Brutus thrashed Julius with a stick, so he cried. From the time he was small he'd been told that crying was something people did when they were sad, but he was often sad, and rarely cried. Today he was making up for that. He cried like no one was watching, because no one was around to watch. It was the honest, undiluted cry of a little boy far from home who had been spared death at the hands of a wolf by dumb luck. When it was over, he stopped hugging his knees and wiped the tears from his face, knowing he would have to wash his mouth and chin when he got to the stream.

As he walked, he felt a pain in his right leg, and he was limping slightly. He'd fallen on it and it was only bruised, but it still hurt. The wolf had also torn his best fur, now soaked with his tears. Parts of it hung off him loosely, and he knew it would neither fit as well nor keep him as warm as it had. At the stream he knelt down and washed off his mouth and chin with the cold water, then splashed more on the rest of his face. As he refilled his water skin, he realized that it was leaking from one corner; when the wolf had bitten down on the fur, it must have bitten through and torn the corner of the water skin.

    Frustrated, Unter became frantic, trying over and over to fold that corner up and tie it to stop the leak. No matter how tight he tied it, the leak continued, and tying it merely made his leaky water skin smaller. He threw it down and laid down on the grass to catch his breath. Sitting up he had an idea; he found a pebble in the stream just slightly larger than the leak, and forced it as far into the broken corner as he could. When he re-filled the water skin, it still leaked, but only a tiny amount. It was the best he could do, so he moved on.

# TRAVELER FROM AN ANTIQUE LAND

An old man sat at a chair surrounded by books and candles. He strained to read the text of a dusty, yellowing book that looked like it should crumble between his bony fingers. The cell door swung open with a loud creak, and Golamel walked in. He walked quickly to the small table and leaned over it, palms down on its surface. "Have you found what I need yet, traveler?"

The old man looked up, revealing the pointed end of his long beard. "I have asked that you call me Hakeem, my lord. You have made it clear I won't be doing much more traveling."

Golamel gave him a sly smile. "I'm a reasonable man. If you do what I want, and traveling is what you want, then you may have much traveling in your future."

Hakeem looked up, stone-faced. "I expect that when I finish what you've asked of me then I will die."

"Don't be silly... Hakeem." Golamel placed a hand on his shoulder. "The stories you tell of your homeland are quite interesting to me. I think I could make great use of those. Both the stories of how the goblins of old bled your land slowly, not wasting it all, as well as how you ultimately overcame them, which was if I remember at the expense of your enemies."

"My country survived. It has a long history of survival. I did not say it was a proud history."

Trust me, old man. If you give me what I want I will promise to let you go. I will have no need to kill you. The whole world will be mine."

Hakeem glanced at Golamel, and then back to the page, the top of which showed a smiling goblin raising his fists in triumph.

# THE BRIDGE

The path became both steeper and harder as it wound upwards into the foothills of the mountains. Not far off he saw smoke from the chimney of one of the farmhouses. He considered knocking on the door and asking for a waterskin, but thought again; they wouldn't like him, he wouldn't like them, and they'd be more likely to force him to go home than to give him a new waterskin.

A number of small paths broke off from what was left of the Great Road; nearly all of them led into caves. Mountain caves were the most dangerous of all, because of Trolls. People claimed all of the caves were interconnected and that people who wandered into them would be sold off amongst the trolls as slave labor or food. Before long, though, he did see one path that did not lead to a cave. As castle horse hoofprints led away on the main path, many human footsteps led away on the smaller path, and Unter decided to take it.

Unlike the main path, this one no longer ascended. It leveled out along the edge of the rock between the mountains, and he could see a bridge in the distance. After the bridge the path rose again, rejoining the main path, with a great deal of distance saved.

Unter picked up his pace but slowed with the bridge nearby, now that he could smell something quite foul. Something wasn't right, though he didn't know what it was. He very slowly crept forward, looking around him again and again. Steep slopes drew away from the path as it neared the bridge. Wails caught his ear and he saw that under the bridge to the right, an enormous net held dozens of people (farmers, by their clothes) suspended in the air.

Unter broke for the bridge in a sprint but it was too late; he could feel it above him, and saw the shadow out of the corner of his eye. Swinging deftly, it landed with the sound of thunder at the base of the bridge. This was larger than any troll he'd ever heard of. His father was a big man, and it was three times his size, grey and hairless, like the troll he'd seen in the valley, but bigger. Very slowly and deliberately it bent at the waist, leaned over, and smelled Unter's hair. Unter closed his eyes. He felt hot, smelly breath. "You ain't one of them, eh?"

"One of them?"

"All them ruddy farmers come running up here and try to cross my bridge runnin' from the dragon. They couldn't pay no toll."

"No. I came on my own."

"Fine then, pay the toll. You *can* pay the toll?"

"Of course I can pay the toll. But I hardly think I should when the bridge can't hold my weight."

The troll furrowed his brow. "Whatchoo talkin' about? This bridge? A little fing like you? If it can hold my weight, you won't have no problem."

"Why should I believe it can hold your weight? I just met you. There's no reason for me to trust you, after all. You could turn people away who can't pay the toll, but you throw them in a net."

"You wanna go in the net yourself?"

"No, certainly not. I only think it's fair you demonstrate the strength of the bridge. Walk out on the bridge and come back and I'll pay the toll."

"This ain't some trick?"

"I can't sneak past you if you're on the bridge."

The troll scratched its head and thought slow thoughts. Finally, it nodded and walked out onto the bridge a few steps.

"Farther."

The troll grunted and continued a few more steps.

"You're not even halfway!"

"So what?"

"If I were going to make a collapsing bridge, I'd make the weak part on the far half." Unter crossed his arms.

"Fine!" The troll lumbered on until he was nearly all the way across the bridge.

"Now spin in a circle!"

"What for?"

"If you do that, I'll be content with the strength of the bridge at the edges!"

The troll grunted with reluctance once again and Unter glanced down where the troll had come from. Next to the base of the bridge was a pulley system held together with ropes. He stumbled down the steep slope and began cutting one of the ropes with his knife.

The troll took a moment to realize that Unter had gone. "Hey? Hey, where'd you go?"

"I'm getting my money out, I don't want you to see how much I have."

"No, this is some trick. Come out!"

Unter did not, and said nothing. The troll began to walk, then to run, his footsteps getting louder and louder. Finally, the rope broke and the bridge flipped, the far end pointing straight down. The troll screamed but could not catch on to anything; it fell into the deep crevasse.

He worked his way to the net and found another system of pulleys. Fearing that cutting the ropes would drop them, he studied the pulleys to see what to do next. He saw that a swing arm was holding them over the crevasse and that it was connected to a single horizontal lever. He tried as hard as he could to push it, but it wouldn't budge. Finally, he backed up and ran at it; the force caused it to move a little, and with it, the swing arm. Repeating this several times, he safely moved the net over solid ground, then cut the ropes. The net fell and the farmers came spilling out of it.

It was a mess; they were crawling all over each other, fighting, punching and kicking. When the last of them had emerged, they began asking where the troll had gone.

"The troll is dead. It fell."

"Can you fix the bridge?" one of them asked. Several others nodded along.

Unter was confused. He'd been expecting gratitude. "I had to cut the ropes to kill the troll. But I'm sure that all of us together could get the pulley back together and—"

One woman looked angry. "Couldn't you have killed it some other way?"

"Like with a lance?" suggested one man.

"I don't have a lance. I didn't come here to kill the troll. I didn't even know there was a troll. All I wanted to do was to cross the bridge."

"All of us wanted to cross the bridge but none of us broke it!" The farmers were now yelling as a mob.

"Wait, wait," said one older woman. "You at least brought food for us?" The mob calmed, and looked at him hopefully.

Unter only became more exasperated. "I didn't know you were here. Isn't saving your lives enough?"

"You break our bridge and leave us here hungry. We were better off with the troll!" The mob yelled in agreement.

"The troll was going to eat you."

"Better troll food than cold and hungry with a broken bridge!" To Unter's surprise the mob still agreed.

"Fine, don't fix the bridge for my sake. But if you still want to cross it, get that pulley working for yourselves."

One small man crossed his arms. "Well that's just great. You break the bridge and get us to fix it, and then you can just cross it like nothing. For free. I think you owe us a toll."

Never looking back, Unter snickered all the way back to the main path.

# PREPARATIONS

"Stand there. Don't move."

Sophia obeyed. She looked around the room at the top of the tower, knowing nothing good was in store for her. Golamel had not hurt her yet, not once, but thought he would if he had to. Never was she greeted by anything approaching either malice or kindness, but indifference. For Golamel, Sophia was an object, not one to be thrown around or abused, but saved. There was no logic to it, but somehow she knew that was the right way to put it. The princess was being saved, saved to be used in some way later. If I wanted to make a cake, she told herself, I would not spoil the eggs.

He had taken care to clean this room, which had been a mess. Marks on the dusty floor showed that things had been repeatedly moved around. Glass in the large window looked new. Two items were the focus of the room: a large wooden pulpit with steps, as if it were made for a small child, and a cross-shaped table with straps. Sophia could only imagine the straps were for a head, arms, and legs, and then she realized why he'd brought her up here.

Golamel fiddled with large lenses near the window. As he lined them up, sunlight focused through the lenses sent a beam toward the cross. He quickly moved them away. A tiny pillar of smoke curled up from the cross. Nodding, he took note of where the lenses had been and how far he'd moved them away from the window. Smiling, he walked over to the cross, looked at Sophia and gestured to the cross. She gulped.

"Relax," he said, shaking his head slightly. "Just a few

measurements and it's back to your room. It's not going to hurt you."

Closing her eyes for a moment, she clenched her fists and walked forward, then climbed onto the cross table and tried to breathe as Golamel adjusted the straps and tightened them. He studied them for a moment, then loosened them. "All done. Now I can take you back to your room."

He led her back there, the only sound their footsteps on the stone beneath them. She was worried, because it was the only time he'd taken her out of her room for any purpose. At no time did she feel like he'd lied to her, after all, the table had not hurt her, and he'd barely tightened the straps at all, dismissing her fears of painful wrists and ankles. It was that he had chosen to say so little. If she was to be strapped to that cross, what was the pulpit for? What did he plan to do with the lenses? What horrible things might be in store for her?

The door slammed shut behind her, and he locked it. She stared out the window and could just make out the castle; a cavalry trumpet echoed in the distance. Hearing it brought muddy memories of a story she hadn't heard since she was very small, about another girl named Sophia, and what had happened to her in that same tower.

# THE LONG WAY

Unter trudged along, cursing the decision he'd made to take the shorter path in the first place. The main path was going to take him much longer than the shorter path would have. While he did not smile at the misfortune of others, when he looked down and saw that the bridge still had not been raised, he felt relief in that coming all the way back had still saved him time.

In the mountains, it was now cold even at midday, and he feared what trying to sleep in this cold might be like. He followed a gradual slope and curve, though there was plenty of room for cavalry, so it was easy going for him. Snow blew here and there off the caps, but the ground was dry for the most part.

Looking down from the high road, the kingdom looked tiny. It did not seem like it should have been such a long walk to the castle, or that to get here should have taken him days. When he looked ahead to the ruined fortress it seemed so close that it ought to have been only a few hours away, but he knew it would take at least another day, perhaps two.

As he neared the junction with the shorter road, he spun around several times when he heard something behind him, but he never saw anything. At sundown he spotted some pines and stopped to make a shelter. He was pleased to find an outcropping of rocks and more pleased to see that it did not lead to a cave; it would be enough room for him, without worry of an animal attack in the night. He gathered the branches he needed to cover the opening and block the wind, and bundled up to go to sleep.

When he woke in the morning, he discovered the source

of the sounds he'd been hearing behind him on the road. Back a few yards from his shelter was another, this one larger and more hastily thrown together. Two pairs of feet stuck out from between the pine branches, but it was large enough to hold more people, and he was sure that it did. As quickly as he could, he gathered his things and moved on, hoping to lose them.

It was the coldest and cloudiest day yet. The wind blew hard, but he was lucky that it was at his back, almost propelling him to his destination. He paced himself less than usual, with a strong feeling that he would reach the ruins that day. Obstacles that would have felt daunting in the previous two days seemed easy now; he vaulted over rocks in the road, ran through snow drifts, and slid forward on icy patches as if it were all a game.

A big curve in the road was where he first saw them. There were four adults, more farmers by their clothes, and he thought he could make out two men and two women, though it was too far to see their faces. He thought they must be some of the farmers from the bridge, but thought again; the mob had been angry with him, so why follow him now? If they were still angry, perhaps they were chasing him in order to hurt him, but it seemed to him to be a lot of work. Perhaps, he thought, they'd wanted to thank him, as he'd expected the farmers to do, but were afraid to in front of the others. There was no way to tell for certain without talking to them, and to do that was to risk harm. Again, he pressed on, as fast as ever.

At last, he came to the place where the road split. Every step took him farther from home than he'd ever been before; for the first time in his life he could see, not as a drawing in a school book, but with his own eyes, land outside of the kingdom. If for only a moment his head emptied of his reasons for coming this way and he imagined thousands more; to travel the whole world and see every country; to learn how to sail on a ship and see every shore. He might become a knight in some other court, spending his days speaking a language he did not yet know, eating strange and exotic foods he'd yet never heard of.

The moment passed and he looked to the shorter, winding

road to the fortress, grandeur gone. But he was astonished to see a light in one of the windows. Unter smiled, knowing now that his theory had been correct. Someone was, once again, occupying the old Goblin Fortress. Seeing that light made it hard not to start sprinting, but he knew it was still too far. Glancing behind him once, he could no longer see the farmers that were following him.

Dusk settled in. Under normal circumstances, he would stop for the night, but the fortress was just too close. With the last of the light fading he began to run. The road wound around to the front of the fortress, where the goblins would stage their raids. As he came around, he could see firelight; many torches lined the drawbridge, and in front of the portcullis sat a fat red dragon.

Sprinting now, he ran out of sight, hiding, pinning himself against the near side of the fortress wall. His chest was heaving. There was no way he could think of to get past the dragon. Was there another way into the fortress? Surely there had to be, if only if it was a hole in the wall. Whoever now inhabited the fortress had done some rebuilding, but much of the outside was still ruins.

Slowly he worked his way around the fortress toward the back. There may have been holes in the walls he could have used higher up, but it was hard in the low light to be sure that they were safe. Finally, he came to what looked like a dry riverbed directly behind the fortress. At the base of the foundation, he saw what he'd been hoping for: a doorway.

The door was round and small, and though it had no handle, it hung open just enough for him to pry it open. He imagined that it was an escape route for the goblins, in case their enemies had breached the fortress, or perhaps it was just an easier way to get inside. It was impossible to know for sure.

As he was about to go inside, he heard shouting.

"Hey! Hey there!" The farmers started waving their arms at him.

"Shhh!" After all the trouble of avoiding detection, he didn't want the dragon coming after him now.

They started running down the slope toward him.

# THE GOBLIN FORTRESS

The back door to the fortress hung all the way open, and Unter stood in front of it. He faced the four farmers who stood speechless. Each of them was covered in dirt from head to toe; their hair appeared brown, but it may have been another color. The dirt made it hard to say. Their clothes were tattered but less dirty than their faces. He could make them out now, and recognized them from the mob. None of them had spoken against him.

The taller of the two men removed his hat and spoke first, as one might speak to a knight, and not to a boy who was small for his age. "My name is Luther, and this is my wife, Marian." He gestured to the woman closest to him, who nodded. "This is William and his wife Harriet." Each nodded in turn.

"My name is Unter. I'm the miller's son. I'm going to save the princess."

The farmers stood silently, dumbstruck. This time William spoke. "Well, I suppose we just wanted to thank you for letting us out."

Unter narrowed his eyes at them. "I appreciate you thanking me, but why didn't you do it before?"

William looked at the ground. "Well, everybody was pretty mad about the bridge."

"Were you mad?"

"Well no—I mean most everybody… maybe everybody but

us, you see, they all seemed to be mad and…"

"You were afraid."

William looked up. "Right, right."

"So, what now?"

"Huh?"

"What do you plan to do now?"

William looked at Luther, who spoke again. "Um, well, I guess we were hoping you could help with that."

"So, you followed me into the mountains with no plan of what to do?"

"You really seemed to know what you were doing."

Unter, exasperated, sighed loudly. "Well, I'm going inside to save the princess. I would suggest you come in to get warm and start home in the morning."

Harriet spoke up. "It's not safe!"

Marian nodded. "A dragon! A dragon chased us from the fields!"

Unter stopped for a moment. "Would you like to help me save the princess?" They looked at each other, smiled and nodded. "Do you have weapons?" Confused, they looked at each other and said nothing. "What exactly do you have?" They shrugged. Unter turned away from them and went inside. The farmers ducked down and followed him.

Inside the fortress was very dark, and while it was warmer than the outside it was still not warm enough for Unter to remove his furs. The farmers had to crouch and often bumped into each other and into the walls. Unter had no idea how long the corridor was, so he just kept going. Finally, he saw a light, and came out in a round room lit by torches. There was a heavy wooden door and a spiral stone staircase leading up.

One by one, Luther, Marian, William and Harriet came spilling out of the goblin corridor, each losing their balance and falling onto the stone floor. As they came out, they warmed themselves by the torches. This room was much warmer than the corridor had been. Luther removed one of the torches from the wall and handed it to Unter, who proceeded up the stairs. He looked back and they hadn't moved; he only shook his head and continued up the stairs. Reluctantly, they began to follow.

At the top of the stairs, he found another large, wooden door. It was very heavy and the handle was too high for him to reach, so he needed Luther to open it. When he did Unter winced at the sound it made; the creak was very loud and he was sure that anyone in the fortress could have heard it, but when he listened for footsteps, he heard none.

They stepped out into the main hall. All but one of the towers had crumbled; large holes in the walls here let wind and snow inside. As he looked toward the front, he could just make out the dragon outside; he continued on across the stone floor toward the tower and the next set of steps.

There had once been another wooden door that opened to the tower, but nothing was left now but a rusty hinge. More torches on the walls lit the way. They passed a few darkened rooms as they climbed; each time, Luther picked Unter up so that he could look into the room, holding the torch at the barred window in each door. He thought of questioning why Luther didn't simply take the torch and look himself, but didn't bother.

At last, they came to a door with light coming from the window. Luther swung it open, but instead of the princess they saw a man at a desk covered in books. He turned around quickly, and that was the last thing they saw.

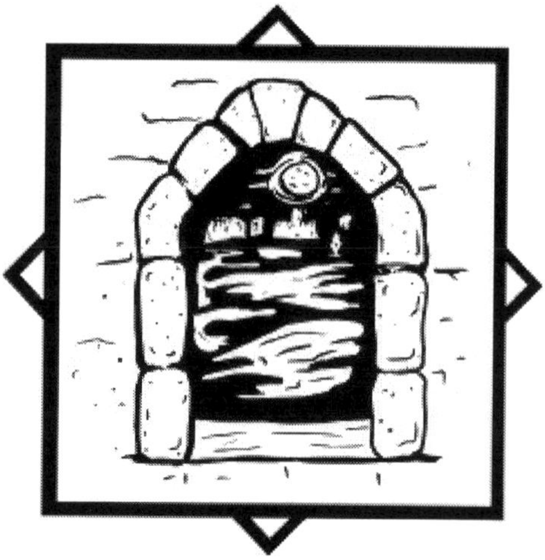

# IN THE DUNGEON

Unter awoke on a cold stone floor. Looking around he saw bars all around him; he was in a cell surrounded by other cells. Each of the farmers was in a cell nearby. He looked down the corridor and saw what he could only imagine was the large wooden door at the bottom of the stairs near the goblin corridor. It must have led to a dungeon.

To his left was a cell with a stranger in it; the old man was sleeping, and Unter could just make out his beard. Unter stood up and looked around, but did not see the princess anywhere. On the floor of the cell Unter found a sliver of metal; he climbed up onto the bars of his cell and began trying to pick the lock.

After several minutes he became frustrated and began banging the door back and forth. "It's no use," said the old man, who had rolled over. "The locks are enchanted." Now the old man sat up, scratching at his hair and beard. "You're only a boy. Tell me, what is your name?"

Unter climbed down and stood on the floor, and took a few steps toward the old man's cell. "Unter."

"Unter." The old man nodded. "My name is Hakeem. Other than the circumstances, I should say I am pleased to meet you. I should wish that we would have met some other way, so that we were not both held prisoner here."

"How long have you been here?"

"It's been a few weeks. Golamel decided at some point that my counsel was too precious to let go."

"Golamel?"

"Yes, the sorcerer. That is his name. Did he not capture you?"

"I only saw him for a moment… in his study."

"Aha. He must have used his powers to bring you down here. They grow every day. And they," he said, gesturing to the still sleeping farmers, "they must be your family?"

"No. I'm the miller's son. They're farmers. I met them on the road and they followed me here."

Hakeem's face lit up with amusement. "They followed you. Of course."

Unter stood tall and straightened his back, puffing out his chest. "I've come to save the princess."

"And come further than anyone yet, it seems. Golamel has her locked up in the tower, in the second-highest room. He's actually complained that the dragon he tasked with guarding the main gate has had nothing to do. The mountain trolls and flying dragons he set about the kingdom have done their jobs too well."

"So they are sorcery? Not real?"

"Oh, make no mistake, young man, so long as his incantations are in place they are as real as you or I, and far more dangerous. How in the world did you get past them?"

"They ignored me."

"Sometimes being very small works to your advantage. But surely the dragon at the gate saw you?"

"I found a doorway in the back. It was small; it was—"

"Goblin-sized."

"Yes."

"Unfortunately, Unter I think that it is too late, that we are all doomed. Golamel is quite angry with this kingdom and has already begun to take what he sees as his just revenge. Tomorrow night he plans to take the biggest steps toward taking over the whole world."

"He's going to try to repeat what the Goblin King did."

Hakeem smiled again. "Yes! Yes! He is repeating the story of your founding. Dark forces take the princess, Sophia, and plan to use her for a dark purpose. This time Golamel feels especially proud. He needed no goblin army to take the princess. But if he succeeds, he will have one, I think."

"The spell creates a goblin army?"

"Actually, there are two major incantations. The first, the Spell of Great Power, would expand his powers further, so that his magical abilities will become much stronger. The second, in sacrificing the princess, would be the Spell of Great Dominion. I have not told him everything that I have learned from the goblin texts. I believe that the Spell of Great Dominion would change every man, woman and child in this whole world into goblins."

"Including us?"

"Including us."

"But what about him?"

"That remains unclear but I have a theory about that too. The goblin text is very unclear about what the Spell of Great Power does, exactly. But afterward begin the references to the Goblin King. I cannot prove it but I believe that Golamel, once he performs the Spell of Great Power, will transform himself into the Goblin King."

"So, in the founding story of Antonia, a sorcerer had already transformed himself into the Goblin King when the princess was kidnapped?"

"Yes, I think so. I believe he had performed smaller spells to change people into goblins, before kidnapping the princess to perform the Spell of Great Dominion. He'd planned to sacrifice the princess on the full moon, but as you know the king intervened. The palace seems blind now to what Golamel is doing; he has been very smart, and they are preoccupied with his monsters."

"How did you learn all of this?"

Hakeem sat back against the bars in his cell. "My kingdom, like so many others, was ravaged by the goblins. It was an ancient kingdom, far from the Lowlands, and we had our own sorcerers. They plotted and decided that they would cast a spell making our kingdom invisible to the goblins. Soon they left us alone, concentrating on our neighbors, most of whom became a part of the goblin army themselves. We survived at their expense. But our scholars have more knowledge of the goblins than most. They are little more than legend in newer kingdoms like Antonia."

"If we get out of here I would like to travel all over, and learn as much as I can."

"You don't want to stay here in Antonia, and become a miller like your father? It's a fine profession."

"No."

# THE BIG DAY

Slivers of dawn crept in through cracks in the walls and some tiny windows, and the farmers woke up. Sore and confused, they struggled to their feet and made their way to the bars of their cells. "What happened?" William asked. "Where are we?"

"A sorcerer put us in the dungeon." Unter didn't turn around.

Luther shrugged. "What are we going to do?"

Unter shook his head. "There's nothing we can do. We can't even pick the locks. He's going to take over the world and there's nothing we can do about it."

Luther's face dropped into a frown. "Nothing?"

Hakeem addressed them. "I've been through all the books he's been using, and other than killing him, reversing his incantations seems nearly impossible to do. The reversal spell for the stronger incantations is long and complicated; for the simpler ones, like these enchanted locks, that he learned when he had little power at all, there is only a vague reference to a song."

Unter turned sharply; Hakeem had yet to mention any song. "Song? A song? What does it say?"

Hakeem seemed rattled. "That's just it, it says almost nothing. It's hard to decipher. It makes reference to simple incantations like those that lock us in our cells, and says they can be reversed with a song familiar to the sorcerer in his youth. It's not as if I can ask Golamel what songs he knew when he was a boy."

"But wouldn't any song work?"

"There's no way to tell without trying it."

"What about the national anthem?" Unter stood erect, holding his breath, his eyes wide, waiting for Hakeem to respond.

Hakeem smiled as if he'd just heard a subtle joke. "Hmm. I'd never thought of that. I'm sure that he heard it as a boy. His anger at this kingdom made it quite clear he was raised here by his family."

Marian rushed to the bars of her cell. "That's wonderful, Unter! Go ahead, sing the song!"

All of a sudden Unter went pale; his breathing became labored, and the world seemed to blur around him. William opened his mouth and said something but Unter could not make it out. He began tugging on his right ear, and walking backward. Stumbling, he hit the floor. As he caught his breath, he shook his head and looked up at William. "I'm sorry, I didn't hear you. What did you say?"

"I asked if you knew the song. Do you know it?"

Unter's eyes widened slightly, and he hesitated before speaking. "Um, no, I can't say I remember the words to the song very well. We learned it in school but I've been away from school for a while, and... I must have just forgotten it."

The farmers looked at each other, a little confused. Shrugging, they began to sing Antonia's national anthem together. Hakeem crawled to his feet as they reached the second verse and the locks began to glow. "Yes! Yes, that's it!" But Hakeem's face changed quickly to horror: "Wait, wait, stop, stop!"

The singing stopped, and the farmers looked at him. Luther put his hands out. "What? It was working, wasn't it?"

Hakeem nodded. "We must be patient. Golamel will be coming soon to bring me to the observatory, where he will order me to help him with tonight's incantations. Once he does that he will be preoccupied. If you wait to release yourselves, you can be sure that he will not find you again. Were he to find you now, I think that he would rather kill you all than have you risk his plans. As it stands, he has no idea you have the power to escape."

William spoke. "Escape? But Unter wants to save the

princess."

"Hakeem is right. I can't do that if I'm dead."

They all sat, waiting very impatiently for Golamel to arrive as Hakeem had said he would. The sky started to darken as the sun went down. Unter started to wonder, had Hakeem been wrong about the day? Perhaps they had more time than he'd thought, and he should get everyone up and convince them to sing the song and get themselves out.

He'd only just stood up when the large door creaked open and Golamel appeared. Sneering, he turned his nose up at Unter and the farmers before facing Hakeem's cell. Turning his hand as if it held a key, the cell door popped open. Hakeem gathered books and moved toward the open door, when William began shaking the door of his cell loudly. "Let us out!" he shouted.

Golamel made a shoving motion in the air with an outstretched hand. "Quiet." William's body crashed against the far wall and he fell to the floor, writhing in pain. Harriet screamed and covered her mouth. Golamel turned around slowly, looking at each of the prisoners, then turned back to Hakeem. "Come on, then."

Hakeem hastened out, arms loaded with books, ahead of Golamel toward the door. With a swing of his arm Golamel opened the door, and once he'd walked through it, the door swung shut again. They heard it lock and it glowed slightly.

Harriet rushed to the door of her cell and frantically began singing the song. Unter urged her to hush, putting a finger to his lips. She stopped singing but her breathing became a hiss, after a few minutes Unter nodded, and Luther and Marian joined Harriet singing the national anthem. After they completed the second verse the cell doors swung open as Hakeem's had. The large wooden door also swung open.

Harriet rushed into William's cell and cradled his head. The other farmers walked in. William was hurt but did not appear to have any broken bones. Unter stood outside. "Get him out of here. Go somewhere safe. Find the cavalry, someone, and call for help." Luther and Marian stood still for a moment, saying nothing.

Finally, Luther nodded. "Good luck to you. Save the princess."

As they made their way toward the goblin corridor, Unter slowly climbed the first set of stairs, being careful to make as little noise as possible. He couldn't say how quickly Golamel and Hakeem would be climbing the steps of the tower, and he didn't want to run into them early. When he reached the top of the stairs the door was shut, and he remembered that it had been a little too high for him to open the last time. He reached for his knife, and to his surprise it was there; Golamel hadn't checked him for weapons when he'd thrown him in the dungeon.

Raising the knife above his head he moved the handle slowly; as he leaned backward the door moved a little, then more. Unter lost his balance and fell backward; he held his breath as the knife fell, point-first, toward him. The blade hit the stone right next to his face and instinctively he covered the side of his face, but the knife had fallen over harmlessly.

Catching his breath he got up, put the knife away, and crept out into the main hall. His feet made loud sounds on the stone floor; carefully he placed his heels on the floor first, then moved to the toes. It slowed him even more, but made almost no sound. He crept toward the tower and looked up. It was filled with torchlights, but he heard nothing.

He moved past the doors they'd seen before, heading for Golamel's study, where he would stop first. Before he reached it, he could see that candles were still lit inside and the door hung open. Silently, he peeked his head into the doorway, only to find a mess; several books had been knocked onto the floor, but otherwise it was empty. Unter looked up the stairs again, and again he saw and heard no sign of them.

When he came to the next doorway it too was both lit and open; he heard nothing, but again could not dare to do more than peek inside. This room, which Hakeem had told him would be the princess's room, was empty except for a feather bed and a few candles. Golamel had already taken her to the observatory.

The remainder of the climb seemed too long; Unter hadn't

remembered the tower being this tall but he pressed on. There were no more doors; the observatory was the last one, and it was situated far above the rest of the fortress. At last, he heard shouting; the first of the light from the doorway was flowing down the stairs now. Lights flickered as someone, probably Golamel, moved about inside. It was his voice now, and he was yelling, impatient. Unter was only a few feet from the door now, the largest door of all, which was open and against the wall.

# THE OBSERVATORY

Unter approached, more tentatively than ever. The shadows, tiny and fleeting just a moment ago, were now ever-present. Hakeem cowered; Golamel, closer to the light, appeared large and monstrous, his features exaggerated. "Hurry, hurry! Come on now, we don't have much time. Now get it on the podium and open it to the right passage. I want to be ready when it starts." Creeping closer he gathered the courage to look inside; both Golamel and Hakeem were now looking away, toward the setting sun. Holding his breath, Unter crept inside and scurried into a shadowy corner of the room.

From the shadows he could see the entire room. Candles and torches were lit along the wall opposite him, from the doorway to the observatory window. An elaborate machine with lenses sat next to the window. Directly in front of it was a cross-shaped table, where he could make out long, blonde hair. He took this to be the princess; when she moved, he was relieved to find that she was still alive. Many books sat piled on a table against the wall, and beside that table were piles of wooden debris, none of which looked important. What Golamel was concentrating on was a podium, one that looked much too small for him. On it sat a huge book, the largest that Unter had ever seen. Hakeem was flipping frantically through the pages.

Hakeem stopped and pointed, chest heaving, to the top of the page. Golamel smiled and clapped his hands together. Then he reached out with his left hand, back behind him, toward the piles of debris, and out came a length of rope, moving like a snake.

It wrapped itself around Hakeem, pinning his arms to him, and tying itself in a knot. Grunting and wailing, he rose in the air for a moment, settling against the wall. "In case you get any ideas."

Unter made his move. With Golamel's back turned Unter rushed him, knife held out in front of him like a sword. As he got within range to strike Unter closed his eyes; he could not help it. He'd never harmed a person before, even if the person was a sorcerer. Nothing happened; when he opened his eyes, he found that the blade of his knife had bent over like grass. He dropped it and looked up to see Golamel staring down at him.

"You again? How'd you get out?"

"Why should I tell you?"

Golamel smiled. "Could you not get your parents out?"

"They're not here."

Golamel looked confused. "Who was in the dungeon, if not your family?"

"I came alone. I met them on the road, and I sent them away. One of them was hurt, and there was nothing they could do to help me."

"*You* sent *them* away." Unter nodded. Golamel smiled again. He came down from the podium and laced his fingers behind his back.

"Where do you come from? Who is your father?"

"I live at the mill. My father is the miller, Cassius."

"And are you named Cassius like him?"

"No, Cassius is my brother, the eldest. There is also Apollo, and my older sister Artemis. I have a baby sister named Penelope. My name is Unter."

Golamel narrowed his eyes. "Your name... it does not match the rest of your family. Why would your mother name you Unter?"

"My mother says I was an ugly and fussy baby. As the ugliest child I got the ugliest name. At least my name isn't *Golamel*."

Golamel laughed at this. "My mother named me Golamel for a similar reason. She said she didn't like the look of me. I had two brothers, Fortimus, who was much older, and the baby, Anthony, like the old king. It seems we were both the odd one out." Unter's face changed just slightly. "How did you get here?"

"I walked. It took me a few days."

"And the dragons?"

"They ignored me. Maybe I was too small to see."

"You came all the way by yourself. Your family didn't try to stop you, or come with you?"

"I told them I was leaving but they weren't really listening. They never do."

"My family didn't listen either. I was a lot smarter than Fortimus, but no one seemed to care about that, especially after my father died. He was big and strong, and became the man of the house. My mother acted like he was king."

"My father's still around, but they treat my oldest brother the best."

"How did you figure it out?"

"It was the story they always told us in school. Everything was so similar, this is the first place I thought of."

"But no one else did."

"I guess it might have been hard for me to think of it too if the dragons had been chasing me around. Or trolls, I heard about those too. They look real enough."

"Are you still in school? Is anyone there as bright as you?"

"The teacher doesn't like me. She says I ruin the stories, that I think too much about them."

"Nobody cares about brains, do they?"

"No."

"Don't you think they deserve what they're getting? Don't you feel like this is justified?"

"You're sending monsters out to kill them."

"Not to kill them, really. Some of them, yes, I suppose. But mostly the castle cavalry. The rest will just be scared. Alone. Like I felt. Do you not feel alone?"

"Yes, but I never set out to make monsters. All I want is to leave them behind."

"What hope do you have of that? You know how this life is. Have you not been told you'll end up laboring for your brother, every day, just because he's the oldest? You're a commoner like me, so you'll never sit at court with Fat Chuck, actually using your brain in some way, even if it's something as boring as counting the money in his beloved treasury."

"I don't know."

"You and I are just alike. Come and join with me! I can teach you. You could be my sorcerer's apprentice. Magic can overcome strength. It's a powerful ally."

"Did it make you a killer?"

Golamel's face became more grave. "When I was a boy I was very unhappy. One day I found a little dog by the road. Most people didn't like me so I assumed the dog wouldn't like me either, but he acted immediately like I was his best friend in the world. When people talked about loving someone, I didn't feel what they were talking about, until that dog. He was with me just about everywhere I went, and was always happy to see me, even if we were only apart for a few hours. One day as my mother was heading to the market, she sent me off to fetch water. I thought nothing of it, this happened all the time. Only when I got back the dog was not there to greet me. That was unusual. So, I went looking for him. I found Fortimus behind the house, and he was hurting the dog, and laughing. I yelled for him to stop, and he threw the dog into the bushes. It ran off."

"'What will you do?' he asked me. 'If you tell mother, she won't believe you. I will say you did it. She already thinks you are odd, and would expect you to hurt animals.' I knew it was true. So, I searched for the dog, never able to find him. But a few days later I slipped poison into my brother's stew bowl. That's when I left."

"That's horrible," Unter said. "Anyone would be angry. But I know what you're planning to do and I can't help you do that. Not even to learn magic myself."

Golamel snarled. "Fine. Have it your way. But step aside. There's nothing you can do to stop me now." Staring again at the book, Golamel started making guttural sounds. At first

Unter couldn't make sense of it, until he realized that Golamel was actually reading the goblin language. The pages glowed, and Golamel gestured wildly with his hands. At last Unter felt a great force lift him from his feet, and the room was filled with light.

# THE GOBLIN KING

The bright light subsided and Unter could see again. He looked around the room and not much had changed, but he no longer saw Golamel. Struggling to his feet, he ran over to the princess. At the base of the cross-shaped table was an ornately decorated dagger; the hilt was covered with emeralds. Unter picked it up and tucked it inside his furs, where he'd kept his knife.

Walking around the table, he made eye contact with Sophia. He'd never seen her close up before. Normally it was at official events, and she'd always looked bored. Now she only looked scared. "Help me," she whispered. "Please."

Hurriedly, he began pulling on the straps, but was unable to loosen them. Golamel had made them too tight to budge. Sophia gasped when he removed the knife but relaxed when he started sawing back and forth on the leather. It wasn't doing much good; the leather was too strong. Getting her out would take a lot of time, and he knew he didn't have it.

Unter stopped short when he heard a low growl from the far corner. Leaving the princess, he stood near the podium, and from there he saw the source of the sound: a small, green-skinned creature, about Unter's height, but with a wider head and thicker limbs. It was dazed but stirring now. Hakeem had been right: the Spell of Great Power had transformed Golamel into the Goblin King. As it stood Unter could see it wore silk vestments, and even a golden crown.

Looking at itself up and down Unter imagined that Golamel's mind was still inside it somehow, and that he may not have known what would happen. It looked confused. Guttural sounds came out of its mouth over and over; maybe it was trying to talk? Reaching up to its head, it felt the crown and grinned, baring a set of gleaming white sharp teeth. With clenched fists it began walking forward and hissing at Unter.

He quickly stumbled backward up the podium steps and held out the dagger between him and the Goblin King. It jumped backward and hissed louder, but did not move forward again. Unter flipped through the pages of the huge book, turning his head to the pages and back to his enemy over and over again. He could make nothing of the book, as it was in another language he could not read.

Unter abandoned the book and shook the dagger at the Goblin King once more, then let his eyes search for Hakeem. "Hakeem, can you speak? Are you alright?"

"Yes," he replied, weakly. "I'm alright."

"Help me, what do I need to do? What does he need for this spell to work?"

"He is going to recite the incantation, and when it's over he is to cut open the breast of the princess, so that moonlight touches her heart."

"Is that what the lenses are for?"

"He doesn't need them, not really, but it would concentrate the moonlight into a beam, that way he could be sure. The book says that the moonlight must shine brightly on the open heart of the most beautiful girl in the land."

Unter's eyes narrowed. "But Sophia isn't the most beautiful girl in the land."

Hakeem was surprised. "What?"

Sophia was insulted. "*What?*"

The Goblin King felt something akin to an emotion, and said "Gwa?"

"Natalia, the woodcutter's daughter, is easily the most beautiful." Unter continued. "I also think you could argue that Morgan, the carpenter's daughter, is prettier as well—"

"—Thank you, thank you," Sophia interrupted, "but I think

that establishing one girl more beautiful is sufficient."

"Look out!" yelled Hakeem, and Unter jumped off the podium just in time as a pile of debris crashed into it. The Goblin King took the opportunity and ran up the steps, turning pages, and began, in the guttural grunting of the goblin language, to recite the Spell of Great Dominion. Unter made attempts to close in but each time was turned away by flying debris, which the Goblin King seemed able to control with less and less concentration.

The first of the moonlight shone through the window. Dodging debris, Unter ran toward the window and pushed over the machine holding the lenses, but they did not break. Undaunted, the Goblin King continued his incantation. The sounds stopped; the Goblin King smiled, and then jumped up and down with delight as a pillar of green smoke rose from the book and spiraled out the window. The moonlight had nearly reached the cross-shaped table.

Unter had little that he could do now. He put the dagger away and climbed up onto the cross-shaped table, Sophia under his feet, and held the dagger out again. The Goblin King righted the lens machine and put it in front of the window. Under the smoke, still pouring out of the book, moonlight came through the lenses and focused into a beam, now at Sophia's legs. She shrieked.

Carefully Unter walked along the table, stepping around Sophia's body, so that he moved along her legs. Now the beam was touching him instead of her. The Goblin King, enraged, leapt at Unter, driving him from the table. It grabbed onto his hands, trying to pull the dagger away from him. Not letting go Unter scrambled to his feet, pushing and pulling, whatever he could do to hold on. He tried kicking at the creature, but it was awkward, and he nearly lost his balance. Several times the Goblin King's teeth snapped at him, even tearing his furs more, but missing his flesh.

The struggle led them back around to the window; when the Goblin King glanced up it saw that the beam was now focused on Sophia's chest. Frantic, it pulled harder than ever, rocking

Unter back and forth. Unter let go of the dagger; the force of pulling back hurtled the creature toward the window where it flipped backward and over the ledge. Screaming, it hurtled toward the ground below.

Unter rushed to the window. He'd wondered if it might transform back into Golamel, if only for a moment, but like the green smoke it simply disappeared. He freed Hakeem, who helped him loosen the straps so that Sophia could get out. Crying, she embraced them both.

# THE JOURNEY HOME

With Golamel gone and his incantations reversed, Unter, along with Sophia and Hakeem, walked out the front door of the fortress. There was no trace of the dragon or of any mountain trolls. They walked in the moonlight along the mountain road for a few hours when they heard hoofbeats.

Heavily armed cavalry arrived. The captain of the castle guard led two dozen men on horseback. His face lit up with surprise. "Your highness! Are you alright?"

She nodded and responded calmly. "I am. These gentlemen freed me from my captor."

The captain's hand went to the hilt of his sword. "Where is he?" His face was grim.

"The sorcerer is dead. Unter killed him."

They captain looked at Hakeem. "Congratulations! You have—"

Hakeem held up a hand. "I am Hakeem. I did nothing. This is Unter." He motioned to him.

The captain's jaw dropped. He climbed down from his horse and removed his gauntlet, placing a hand on Unter's shoulder. "What were you doing up here all by yourself?"

"I came to save the princess."

"What happened?"

"What happened? I *saved* the *princess*."

Sophia smirked and shook her head.

They rode through the night back to the castle. The guards led Unter and Hakeem to beds where, exhausted, they fell immediately to sleep.

In the morning they were given hot baths and prodded by dozens of guards, scribes and court advisors to retell the entire tale. He was reunited with Luther, Marian, William and Harriet, who had been bathed, fed and given new clothes. They had already regaled the guards with the tale of how Unter had killed the bridge troll with his wits alone.

The king dispatched a carriage for Unter's family, and when they arrived it was his mother who greeted him, with equal measures of glee and embarrassment. "There's my boy. We are so proud of you. But we were... so worried. Where could he be? I think we all thought the worst, with dragons and trolls everywhere we... just didn't know what to think." Her laughter was nervous. She hugged him as hard as he could remember her ever hugging him.

Cassius the elder crouched and patted him on the shoulder. "My son saved the princess." He then kept opening his mouth and closing it again, but said no more. Cassius the younger mussed Unter's hair, but said nothing. Artemis, holding Penelope, paid him no attention as usual; she only sneered, looking around the castle. Apollo disappeared into the crowd, trying to woo the finely dressed ladies.

He met the king and queen privately. Acting as he thought he should, he bowed gravely, saying nothing, but they threw away formalities and hugged him harder than his mother had. "You brought our daughter back to us," the king said through tears, his fat belly jiggling.

"You're a hero," said the queen.

There was a huge ceremony in the castle's great hall that night. Nearly the entire kingdom was in attendance. Unter noted quickly how his mother Helen used every opportunity to brag to her friends and show off the new clothes the family had been given for the occasion. Hakeem and Unter kneeled at the front of the room, where the king and queen sat on thrones, Sophia between them.

The king and queen led the crowd in the national anthem;

Hakeem smirked as he watched Unter mouth the words. The king stood. "To Hakeem, the traveler, we grant you the honor of this medal, for great service to Antonia." He placed a heavy gold medal around Hakeem's neck. "Rise." Hakeem rose, and waved to the crowd, who clapped excitedly.

"Finally," the king said, "for the man of the hour. Unter left the safety of his home and traveled the entire length of our kingdom, through the mountains where he freed dozens of trapped farmers and killed a dangerous troll, into the old goblin fortress, where he outdueled a sorcerer, bent on turning us all into trolls ourselves. This young man left to save the princess. He ended up saving the world." The king removed his sword. "I dub thee *Sir* Unter, Goblinslayer, Guardian of Antonia. Rise."

Unter stood and the crowd erupted with clapping and cheers, whistling and shouting. The king continued, and Unter turned to face him. "You are in our debt. Is there anything your family needs? I understand your father is the miller, is that right?"

"Yes, sire. His mule is getting old, I think he could use another." Cassius blushed.

"Is that all you would ask? A mule?"

"For my family. But I don't want to work in the mill." The crowd whispered to each other; Helen froze with embarrassment. "My brother Cassius is the eldest. He will inherit the mill. That's fine with me, it's what he wants. But I don't want to work for him. I want to be educated."

"Educated?" the king asked.

"Yes. As a commoner my schooling would end in only a few years. I want no titles of nobility, but the education of nobility. I am told that nobles continue schooling until they are adults. They get to travel the world and see all kinds of places and things. I want to do that—I want to travel the world, and to learn."

The crowd was silent. The king looked to the queen, who gestured to Hakeem. "Hakeem, you yourself are a world traveler. If we were to furnish you with a carriage, horses, supplies, books… would you continue this young man's education, and take him with you in your travels?"

Hakeem bowed. "I would be honored."

Sophia raised a finger.

"Oh, yes. One more thing," said the king, who sat down.

Sophia stood up. "Unter, I owe you my life. I think you deserve at least one more thing. A kiss." The crowd gasped. Unter looked nervous. "But not from me."

Unter, and most of the crowd, looked very confused. Emerging from the front row came Natalia, the woodcutter's daughter, wearing a simple blue dress. Sophia winked at Unter, who turned bright red. Natalia, several years older than Unter, towered over him. Her shining black hair had been done up with pearls, likely by Sophia's handmaidens. When she smiled her glittering green eyes captivated him. Unter gulped; when she leaned over, held Unter's head, and pressed her lips to his, the crowd cheered again. Smiling uncontrollably, he fussed with his ears and his hair, chest heaving.

There was a party all through the night. Over and over the king asked Unter to retell parts of the story, in particular the encounter with the wolf and the death of the Goblin King. Most of the kingdom slept in the great hall; when they awoke, Hakeem and Unter were taken by carriage to his family's house so that he could gather his things.

# SIR UNTER, KNIGHT AND WORLD TRAVELER

When they'd all arrived, Unter's parents took him aside to speak to him alone. Helen did most of the talking. "Unter, how could you embarrass us like that? You tell the entire kingdom that you don't want to work for your brother?"

"I told the truth."

"Well… sometimes… you can't just tell the truth, not so plainly like that. Our family's reputation is at stake. What does it say when a boy wants to go traveling the world like that?"

"I thought everyone wanted to travel the world."

"Well, they don't, do they? They take their family obligations seriously. How can you be so selfish?"

"Helen," said Cassius calmly, "he didn't have to get us a mule. If not for him there would be no mill. Just a bunch of yammering goblins."

Helen closed her eyes and swallowed hard. She crouched so that she was at Unter's eye level. "You really want to go?"

"I love you, but yes. I really want to go."

His parents hugged him, each in turn, and it occurred to him that he couldn't ever remember his parents paying him this much attention. But still he gathered his things and joined Hakeem in the carriage. As he waved goodbye to his family, his house, and the mill, a thought occurred to him. "Hakeem," he asked, "if I am so much like Golamel, do you think I will end up like him?"

"No, Unter, I do not think that is likely at all."

"Why?"

"For every way you are like him there is a way you are not. He asked you to join him, he offered you power, and you turned it down. You did the harder thing, and did what you came there to do. Golamel never would have done that. Like you, he was very clever; like you, he was mistreated; like you, he was lonely; like you, he had his reasons to want bad things to happen to others. But he always took the easy way, and in the end all he wanted was power, all he wanted was to hurt people. Your choices led you elsewhere. By doing something no one else could, you found a way to get what you want, and you helped people instead of hurting them. I think that it would be a strange life indeed that ended with you in Golamel's shoes."

The carriage passed the castle, and he saw Sophia waving from a window, and waved back. As the carriage climbed into the hills that led into the mountains and ultimately out of Antonia, he felt a chapter in his life come to a close. But all his life he would remember what spurred him to become the man he would ultimately grow up to be: it was saving the princess.

# THE END

Made in the USA
Middletown, DE
12 March 2023